# Bear's Birthday
# L'anniversaire de l'Ours

## Stella Blackstone
## Debbie Harter

Barefoot Books

**Bear has blown up ten big balloons.**
**His party guests will be here soon!**

10

L'Ours a gonflé dix grands ballons.
Ses invités vont bientôt arriver!

**Bear opens the door to welcome his friends.
He's hoping his day of fun never ends.**

9

L'Ours ouvre la porte pour accueillir ses amis.
Il espère que son jour de divertissement ne finira jamais.

**The first game they play is hide-and-seek.
Where is Bear? Can you see his feet?**

8

Le premier jeu qu'ils jouent est le cache-cache.
Où est l'Ours? Peux-tu voir ses pieds?

Next they all play musical chairs.
There's not enough room for so many bears.

7

Ensuite ils jouent tous aux chaises musicales.
Il n'y a pas assez de place pour autant d'ours.

The group hunts for treasure among the trees.
Bear crouches down: guess what he sees!

6

Le groupe chasse au trésor parmi les arbres.
L'Ours s'accroupit: devine ce qu'il voit!

Bear unwraps the treasure and looks inside.
He has a wonderful birthday surprise!

L'Ours déballe le trésor et regarde dedans.
C'est une surprise d'anniversaire magnifique!

**It's full of delicious jam and honey:**
**Raspberry, strawberry, apricot, cherry.**

4

Voilà du miel et des confitures délicieuses:
de framboise, de fraise, d'abricot, de cerise.

**The table is covered with tasty treats.
It's time for Bear's big birthday feast!**

Sur la table, il y a plein de gâteries savoureuses.
C'est l'heure du grand festin d'anniversaire
de l'Ours.

Bear blows out his candles with one big puff.
When he slices his cake, there's just enough.

2

L'Ours éteint ses bougies avec un grand souffle.
Quand il coupe son gatêau, il y en a juste assez.

"Goodbye, Bear, and thank you," his visitors say.
"We've all had lots of fun today!"

1

« Au revoir, l'Ours, et merci », ses invités disent.
« Nous nous sommes bien amusés› aujourd'hui! »

# Counting Balloons

## Who is making the balloons disappear?
## Can you help Bear count down from 10 to 1?

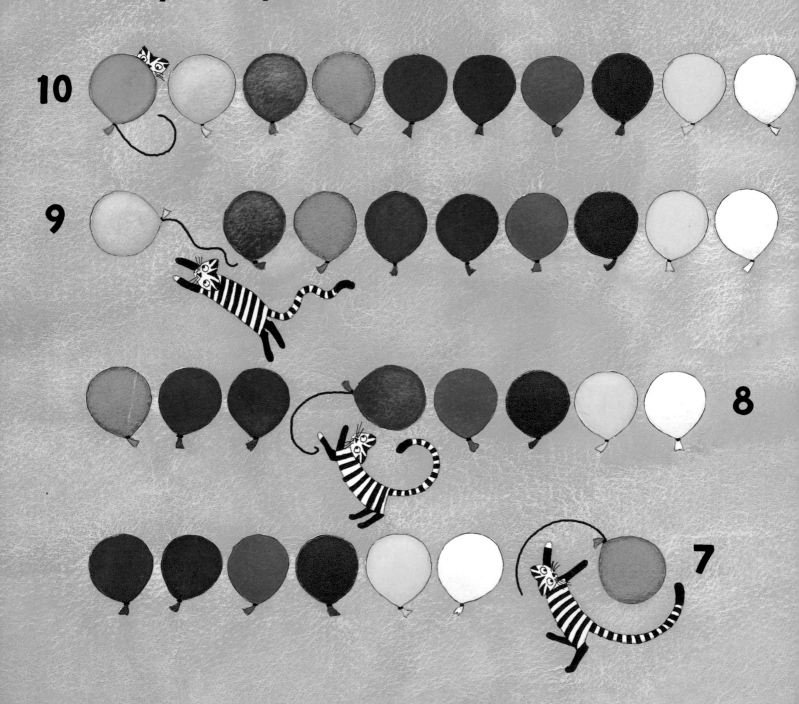

# Compter les ballons

## Qui fait disparaître les ballons?
## Peux-tu aider l'Ours à compter à rebours de 10 à 1?

# Vocabulary / Vocabulaire

one – un

two – deux

three – trois

four – quatre

five – cinq

six – six

seven – sept

eight – huit

nine – neuf

ten – dix

Barefoot Books
294 Banbury Road
Oxford, OX2 7ED

Barefoot Books
2067 Massachusetts Ave
Cambridge, MA 02140

Text copyright © 2011 by Stella Blackstone
Illustrations copyright © 2011 by Debbie Harter
The moral rights of Stella Blackstone and Debbie Harter have been asserted

First published in Great Britain by Barefoot Books, Ltd
and in the United States of America by Barefoot Books, Inc in 2011
This bilingual French edition first published in 2013
All rights reserved

Graphic design by Judy Linard, London and Louise Millar, London
Reproduction by B & P International, Hong Kong
Printed in China on 100% acid-free paper
This book was typeset in Futura and Slappy
The illustrations were prepared in paint, pen and ink, and crayon

ISBN 978-1-84686-944-0

British Cataloguing-in-Publication Data:
a catalogue record for this book is available from the British Library

Library of Congress Cataloging-in-Publication Data
is available upon request

Translated by Elizabeth Parker

1 3 5 7 9 8 6 4 2